TALES OF
IMAGINATION

EVERYTHING IS REAL

DIAMOND MIKE WATSON

ISBN 978-1-891665-49-3

Moon Over Mountains Publishing
1528 Brookhollow Drive, Suite 200
Santa Ana, CA 92705 U.S.A.
800-667-4440

www.WhyMomDeservesADiamond.com
www.GalleryOfDiamonds.com
www.DiamondWatson.com
www.FlyUpFoundation.com

Cover-
Title design by Sean Wright.
Umbrella scene from the 2016 FlyUp presentation at Wilson Elementary in Santa Ana, CA. Photo by Carmen Watson. Illustrated by Ra Avis.

Interior pages-
Illustrated by Diamond Mike and Michaela Watson.

Also by Diamond Mike Watson:

Moon Over Mountains - The Search for Mom
The Legend of Why Mom Deserves a Diamond
Adopted Like Me – Chosen to Search for Truth, Identity, and a Birthmother
In Search of Mom – Journey of an Adoptee
Why Mom Deserves a Diamond - 1993- Essay Winners
Why Mom Deserves a Diamond - 1994- Essay Winners
Why Mom Deserves a Diamond - 1995- 391 Essay Winners
Why Mom Deserves a Diamond - 1996- 732 Essay Winners
Why Mom Deserves a Diamond - 1997- 1,002 Essay Winners
Why Mom Deserves a Diamond - 1998- 1,500 Essay Winners
Why Mom Deserves a Diamond - 1999- Seventh Anniversary Edition
Why Mom Deserves a Diamond - 2000- A Millennium Mother's Day Tribute
Why Mom Deserves a Diamond - 2001- The Greatest Contest on Earth
Why Mom Deserves a Diamond - 2002- 10th Anniversary
Why Mom Deserves a Diamond - 2003- The Legendary Contest
Why Mom Deserves a Diamond - 2004 - Twelve Years of Love
Why Mom Deserves a Diamond - 2005- Words of Love
Why Mom Deserves a Diamond - 2006- Beyond the Goddess Venus
Why Mom Deserves a Diamond - 2007- Sparkling Treasures
Why Mom Deserves a Diamond - 2008- The Crystal Heart
Why Mom Deserves a Diamond - 2009-The Encouraging Branch
Why Mom Deserves a Diamond - 2010- Discovered With Great Bliss
Why Mom Deserves a Diamond - 2011- Legacy Edition
Why Mom Deserves a Diamond - 2012- A Gift of Love

Self portrait in ink. Age 21.

Table of Contents

Acknowledgments

Thanks to:

My beautiful wife, Maria del Carmen, and daughters Patricia and Michaela.

My Mom, Martha Velia Watson. I love you because you first loved me.

My executive assistant, Ra Avis, for editing this book.

Introduction

Since I was a child, I have always enjoyed creative writing. It has always excited me to take a simple thought and bring it into existence with words. Words have the power to inspire, encourage, and even heal. Words evoke thought, and I enjoy leaving others with a sense of wonder by inviting them to question every aspect of life they may have taken for granted.

I am proud to have promoted the art of creative writing in the curriculum of the school system through the Why Mom Deserves a Diamond® contest. Originally in honor of my adoptive mother and the birthmother I had never known, the contest is now in honor of all moms, and provides a vehicle for hundreds of thousands of kids to show appreciation for their moms while sharpening their writing skills.

The contest, which began in 1993, has launched my own desire to express wonder with words. As adults, our puerile thoughts of unlimited possibilities seem to disappear. This has motivated me to reach deep and revive my childhood visions of success, love, and imagination.

Some may say these stories happened in real life. Others will say they only happened inside the abyss of my fantasies. In either case, one may agree that, in one way or another, every story in this book *happened*.

Studies may one day show that being awake or being asleep may not be complete opposites. Whether in living or in dreaming, we all embrace a glowing ember of genius. I hope these stories will help blow life into the ember of every reader.

From deep in the brain, there lies a secret place where everything is real.

The Anniversary Ring

"You love birds can sit here with me if you want," the elderly man said to the young couple desperately looking for a vacant breakfast table. "I'll be leaving soon, and it looks like these are the last empty chairs in the house."

The Garden Terrace was a romantic spot that peered across the Pacific in Laguna Beach. The small tables were each surrounded by four French-styled chairs swirled with wrought iron. The Sunday morning sun reflected brightly against the blue ocean through the viewing windows. The room was cozy and ornamented with rich, dark woods and old hanging portraits of the restaurant's heritage.

"Are you sure?" asked the young man after pulling his sunglasses up over his head. "Aren't you waiting for somebody?"

"I am waiting for my wife, but sometimes she gets distracted and ends up somewhere else."

"Why thank you, sir," the young lady responded. "We should have called earlier for reservations. This is our favorite getaway from our hectic lives."

"Please, sit down. It is important to enjoy life and appreciate everything the universe gives us. Plus, I'm sure you already know their crab avocado omelet is pure paradise." The old man was dressed a few notches better than what was required of the restaurant, but was nevertheless handsome with a black bow-tie showing a trace of the small, metal clamp that held it in place.

The couple glanced at each other for approval, then happily sat and shuffled their chairs closer to the old man. He would be leaving soon, anyways. He appeared to have a small swallow of coffee left in his cup and the bill was placed neatly beside his saucer. His side of the table was spotless without a trace of a stray breadcrumb.

"When you two gonna get married?" the old man asked as the waitress distributed menus and lowered a plate of steaming hot bread on the table.

"We're already married," the two said almost at the same time.

"Today's our third anniversary," the young girl beamed. "We got married in the gazebo right on top of that hill." The girl pointed upward out the window to the right.

"Really?" the old man said with surprise. "I guess that is a popular spot because that is where Zella and I got married!"

"You've got to be kidding," the young man said.

"Nope. Zella and I wanted a small wedding. It was just her, the minister, and me. I suppose God was the official witness. We paid the minister extra to follow us down the steps to the beach to snap a few pictures of us and the ocean background. Zella's dress gleamed in the sun as she sat on one of those big rocks. She smiled so big in the photograph but I'm sure it was not the most comfortable seat."

"That is so romantic," the young lady said. "How long ago was that?"

"Fifty years ago today, but every time I look at that old gazebo, I feel like it was yesterday. This is where we eat breakfast every year."

"What an amazing story!" The young man said. "Are you sure she is not lost?"

"Oh, heavens, no," the old man replied while straightening his bow. "With all the places to shop around here, it's no wonder she always gets side-tracked. After all, it gives me time to prepare my speech."

The young couple looked at each other and smiled. "Are you going to give her a lecture on the virtues of timeliness?" the young girl asked.

"Nope. I'm going to tell her how she is the most important ingredient of my life. Even more wonderful than any crab avocado omelet. And, I'm going to give her this." The old man fetched a small box from his jacket, and carefully raised the hinged lid. Inside rested a glittering diamond perched on a six-pronged platinum pedestal. The diamond was at least twice as large as the young girl's, and projected intense beams of yellow and magenta light from its facets.

"Wow," the young man exclaimed. "I bet she wouldn't be shopping if she knew that rock was awaiting her."

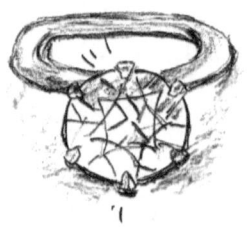

"This is what I wanted to give her fifty years ago, my dear sir, but who had money in those days? Tomorrow never comes. You will learn this soon enough, young man. It is never too late to let someone know you love them. Don't wait until tomorrow to hug your child, to embrace your wife, and to appreciate others. You cannot buy love, but this ring will be a symbol of my love. Every time Zella glances down at her hand, she will remember every great moment we had together." Then the jolly man looked down at the gem and jested. "I sure hope I ordered the right finger size."

"I wouldn't care if it rolled all around my finger," the girl laughed. "That's what rubber bands are for." The young girl turned toward her husband and winked. "That's exactly the size of rock I want, my dear."

"Absolutely, my love," the man began. "And that's exactly what I was planning on giving you forty-seven years from now."

"Well, I guess I'd better check on Zella," the old man said after leaving some cash by his saucer. "I try to have a habit of holding Zella's hand every time we go out. Whenever I let go, she goes shopping."

"Have a wonderful day," the young man said. "Maybe one of these days we'll get a chance to meet your lovely wife."

"I'm sure you will, sir. I'm sure you will." The man straightened his bow once again, ambled out of his chair, and scooted away.

"Will you love me forever like that?" the young girl asked her husband.

"Yes, my love. But it looks like I'd better start saving in order to fulfill your diamond dreams."

"Are you ready to order?" the waitress asked.

"Two plates of your famous crab avocado omelet," the young man said.

"Coming right up. I do hope Mr. Wesley was not bothering you."

"He was charming and hilarious," the young lady said. "I just hope he finds his wife before she buys everything in Laguna Beach."

The waitress gently placed a glass pitcher of iced water on the table. The sun poured brightly onto the container, and crystals of light glinted from the exterior droplets. "Did he show you the ring?"

"Yes," said the young girl. "Thanks to that man I know exactly what I want for my birthday."

"He has wanted to give her that ring for such a long time," the waitress said solemnly. "I hope nobody tries to rob that poor old man. She died from a heart attack right before their fiftieth anniversary. He has come here for coffee every year, on their anniversary, for the past ten years."

I am Sworn to be Your Servant

The Zafcat raised its giant claw for the single slash of Daniel's throat when Eve came from behind and penetrated the hairy beast with her sword. "I am sworn to be your servant," Eve said to Daniel, standing over the slaughtered Zafcat.

For an orphaned slave girl, Eve possessed an unnatural beauty and grace, even in battle. She kept her long black hair tucked under her helmet and her cheeks were always blushed from the cold winds of Landmar. Her armor outlined the shape of her breasts, and her eyes glinted with determination and wonder. After Daniel rescued her from her captives, Eve vowed to be a lifetime follower and friend.

Daniel was a notable diamond merchant who spent his life searching for precious gems. Ancient volcanoes exploded the crystals through their pipes and deposited the gems in the deep river streams. As a child, Daniel's father told him stories of peasants who found fine quality crystals and sold them for an amount that forever changed their destinies. If one searched hard enough, and could hold their breath long enough, a white gem would surely be found. Daniel had gained fame by the time he reached his current age of twenty-five for discovering a two-hundred-carat diamond and negotiating a price of 800,000 Landmara's from the king.

Now word was out that he had discovered a much larger stone. It was a rare Ice Clear flawless, and was so white it glowed bluish in the sun. Daniel knew that wealth meant power, and if he desired, would be able to build a castle from the sale of the stone.

The Zafcat was unleashed by the Carmarians, a tribe that would much rather rob and kill Daniel for his gems than search for the crystals themselves. Time was running out, and Daniel had to seek safety.

"I am sworn to be your servant."

Eve was a woman of few words but was faithful and sincere. Daniel had not intended to fall in love with her, and found it increasingly difficult to hide his feelings. He dared not to express the words of love that would constantly play in his mind.

Liquid granite forms
The body of Venus
Her smooth face is
Chiseled perfection
A poem breathes within her
Yet her eyes
Penetrate my soul
And her lips are music
I yearn for her to become real
And I will run through
Golden fields with my goddess, Eve

"To the North cave!" Daniel forced himself to erase his poetic

frame of mind. Together, they raced to the secret hideaway Eve had discovered. Eve knew that Daniel possessed an enormous crystal that contained the wealth of nations. She was worried that time itself would be the only delay between the safety of Daniel and an army of ruthless Carmarians.

"I am sworn to be your servant." Eve pointed north and made a jerky turn toward Daniel. Daniel couldn't help noticing the captivating beauty of her eyes. He patted his pocket and the lump of the giant stone assured him it was safe. He had tied the gem tightly in the skin of a weasel and attached the skin to his cloak.

As they neared the cave, another Zafcat raced towards Daniel and Eve as they lifted their swords. The Zafcat lunged into the air with its fang-like claws and briefly shielded Daniel from the bright sun. Eve dove under the beast just in time to pierce the animal through its heart. Sadly, the monster had already grabbed Eve by her exposed throat with its talons, and Eve and the Zafcat both died quickly.

Daniel wept as he squeezed Eve's body next to his. Eve had given his life meaning and purpose, and he intended share his wealth with her. The possession of the world's largest diamond would mean nothing without a companion to enjoy life's moments.

"Ricky, dinner's ready!" Mom startled Ricky as he stared blankly at the television screen. Ricky held back a tear, for it was he who had fallen in love with Eve. He thought about her in the daytime, and dreamed about her in the nighttime.

"I'll be right there, mom." Ricky was heartbroken because

Eve died, but still clicked "X" on the remote control to retrieve her sword, animal pelt, boots and sword. As she lay almost naked on the cold ground, he realized he had just scored 1,000 points. Time was running out, and Daniel had to teleport to the final level of the game and sell the diamond to the king.

Heaven Lives Inside Our Hearts

Even when I shield my eyes
I see all beauty in my mind
And though I warmly cuff my ears
A melody I sweetly hear

A paradise lives deep inside
With peaceful streams and trees
Eternal rainbows arch above
And paint the sky for me

A perfect world at my command
Is this a Grand Design?
Or is it just one Giant Thought
That's formed inside my mind?

An inner calm I always find
Her arms of love, all things defined
A planted seed, a tiny voice
That's grown so loud, I have no choice

Now everything that touches me
Brings joy and deep tranquility
I am a drop of consciousness
In every endless sea

Serenity is all around
You first must close your eyes
To know the universe gives love
Makes all of us alive

I hope you see, as morning starts
That heaven lives inside our hearts
An awesome thing about each day
Is we create it along the way

The Mad Child Scientist

"Miss Jenkins found a cockroach in her house, today," said Marcus Wilson's mom as she peeked outside through the curtains.

"Are they bad?" asked Marcus.

"Oh heavens, Marcus, cockroaches are filthy and dirty and carry germs. Do you remember the time we found one on our front porch? If you ever see one, Marcus, stomp it and kill it."

Marcus loved all six-legged creatures, but didn't realize there was such an evil bug.

Being a fairly good student in the sixth grade, Marcus would utilize what he learned from Mr. Rogers' class to kill roaches. During science, Mr. Rogers demonstrated how mixing baking soda and vinegar in a bottle could blast a cap all the way to the ceiling. There would have to be a con-coction, or a poison, that a cockroach could dine on just before flying to that big bug heaven in the sky.

As soon as Marcus's mom descended into the basement to do the laundry, Marcus scooted a chair next to the kitchen sink and hopped on. He commanded full access to the cupboards above and the bottles around the sink.

Marcus had never before seen such an elevated view of the kitchen. He was now as tall as the refrigerator and his dad, who would be proud of his invention when he came home from work.

Marcus was a mad scientist, summoning full control of his laboratory. He decided he'd have to devise a trap for the horrible beast. He would invent something tantalizing on the front porch that the cockroach would eat before attempting to enter the house. Yes, the cockroach would have to believe the poison was just food.

Since the cockroach was found in Miss Jenkins's bread drawer, Marcus was certain the insect loved to feast on bread. Marcus grabbed one of his mom's favorite china plates with the purple and silver rim. This would act as a welcoming mat by the front door. Marcus dropped crumbs of bread from a loaf nearby and sprinkled it all around the rim.

The poison would go in the middle of the plate, but first the roach would have to nibble on the bread and become trapped. Marcus poured a ring of liquid dish detergent inside of the bread. The thick, sticky substance would first trap the bug's legs, and force the bug to slide into the killer poison in the middle of the plate.

Marcus felt pride devising such a genius invention. No roach, no matter how big, could escape the deadly Wilson trap.

The clothes washer and dryer rumbled in the basement. Marcus did not consider himself victorious until he developed the final elixir of death. He opened the cupboard to his left. There was a box of opened baking soda and a flask of vinegar. The cupboard to the right offered a bottle labeled rubbing alcohol.

Marcus plopped ten tablespoons of baking soda in the center of the saucer. Then he poked a hole in the mountain of white powder and filled the volcanic structure with a lake of alcohol. Finally, he poured a large jigger of vinegar into a paper cup and slid it close to but not touching the combustible powder. When the roach slid toward the center, the ingredients would mix together and vaporize into venomous fumes. Bye bye roach. Marcus gave a crazy laugh, wondering why no one ever thought of this before.

The steps of his mom returning up the stairs startled Marcus and he bumped the plate. He wasn't sure if his mom would be angry or proud.

"Marcus, what are you doing standing on the chair?" his mom yelled. "And what's bubbling on my good china?"

Marcus noticed the accidental chemical reaction. "Uh, Hi, Mom, I'm making a poison to kill roaches." Marcus tried to hide the evidence and began stirring the foaming mixture, but it only became a vortex of death, shooting poisonous alcohol fumes into the air.

Marcus's mom observed the opened bottles next to him, and spanked him twice on his flanks. "Do you want to poison yourself, Marcus? Get off that chair and don't ever do that again!"

Marcus raised his arm with a combination of victory and tears and yelled, "But mom, it's in the name of science!"

"Marcus, you could have poisoned yourself. What have I told you about staying away from these things?"

Marcus's mom threw the saucer into the sink and flushed it with water. The Wilson trap would have been the world's most efficient roach killer. Marcus knew that for sure.

Many Words Rhyme with Purple

Many words rhyme with purple
Like durple, turple and magurple

I pour a slurple
Take a glurple
Pardon me, I made a burple

Chicks go chirple
Snakes go sshnurple
My friends are Wurple and Nurple
Ever see a flying flurple?

Hurple, skurple,
To hobble is to hirple
Everyone has made a blurple
(Let's not forget my Uncle Urple)

Mine and yourpel
His and herpel
It's time to feed my little gerpel

I am certainly shurple
I love drizzling murple
On delicious hot klurple

Although there is no such word as zurple
Many words rhyme with purple

Amazing Alexandra

Connor Cruz jumped off the bus onto a mustard-coated hot dog that someone dropped in the parking lot of the Orange County fair. It wasn't the most pleasant way to begin the day, but the salty ocean breeze of Southern California flowed fresh into his nostrils and purified the smell of Budweiser and stale urine from the dirty bus.

Connor entered the fairgrounds and headed toward the bacon-wrapped turkey legs. That's where his girlfriend, Danielle, said she would meet him. The billowing smoke made his eyes water. The sun beat down hard and he became aware of his headache.

He knew he was superstitious, but he had to see Amazing Alexandra. She was the robot fortuneteller that came every year to the fair. His friends said she would always accurately predict their future, especially if you knew the time you were born. Danielle thought he was crazy, and didn't want him to waste money on the rusty contraption. But he needed to know. He needed someone other than Danielle or his friends to give him a new direction in his life.

Ka-BUM, Ka-BUM BUM!

The drums of a female quartet pounded into everyone's ears. No instruments, no vocals, just four young girls banging on what seemed like garbage cans and paint buckets. His head split further.

"My bus was late. See you in 30 mins," Danielle texted.

Connor had to move away from the smoke. The fair-goers provided free entertainment with their marching freak parade of tasteless tattoos and exposed anatomies. One girl sported a lizard kissing a snake on her back. Another flaunted mismatched seamed stockings and a garter belt. An overweight boy was munching on a turkey leg by the wooden tables. As Connor walked behind him, he saw three inches of parting buttocks rising above his jeans.

An orgy of scents fused together- coconut oil from some beach girls, fried chocolate-covered strawberries and sweet cigars. In three steps he detected the aroma of cinnamon funnel cakes and smoked bratwurst. The rotating Cosmic Crush ride slung screaming teenagers mercilessly into the sky.

"Be there in 15 mins. Don't gobble up all the turkey legs," Danielle texted.

As Connor shuffled through the crowd he turned and Amazing Alexandra was looking right at him. The management must have scooted the unpopular attraction alongside the face-painting booth. Connor had ten minutes to spare, and knew this was his opportunity to spend quality time with her.

He inserted his bills and followed the prompts:

Date of Birth: February 25
Sex: Male
Place of Birth: Indianapolis
Time of Birth: 2:32 AM

The machine sputtered and Alexandra's eyes glowed. "Thank you," she said in a mechanical voice. He would never forget his mother telling him he was born on a freezing Tuesday morning at 2:32 AM. A light flashed saying, "Place hand on blue button."

Connor did as commanded. A blue light began to glow through his fingers. The machine began with a high-pitched squeal. His mother had always preached that he could do anything in life. He knew he could make great things happen in the world but he needed validation.

Alexandra descended to a low rumble. A blue cardboard ticket spat from the machine with the date and the fair's logo. Connor flipped the card over and read the fortune:

"Dearest Connor, look around you."

How did she know his name was Connor? He never typed his name. He turned to see if someone was playing a trick on him, but no one seemed to notice he was standing next to Alexandra. Each fair-goer continued to walk aimlessly as if they were characters in their own world.

Connor continued reading. "Everything you see is born from your mind. It is you who can summon the beauty of your world. Always remember, Connor, the awesome thing about every day is you create it."

That's true, he thought. We define our joy by the way we react to situations. When something "happens," it is only relative to the observer. Feelings of love and reverence can be feelings of fear to another. Happiness to one may be anxiety for someone else. Perhaps we create what "happens" from within ourselves.

Connor dizzily stuffed the ticket into his pants pocket. He glanced again to see if someone was watching. Maybe Alexandra was right. Maybe we do create our world. Maybe the things we see are simply how we perceive them. Maybe nothing really exists until we observe. Connor gazed at the trees in the distance. If he squinted he could make them greener. He inhaled deeply and the air smelled fresher. The sounds of the fair became more peaceful. People were beautiful. He was beautiful.

Then Alexandra spoke again with her robot voice. "Dearest Connor. I am so pleased to meet you." Connor stared at Alexandra with his eyes and mouth wide open. "I have been waiting for a long time. Since you were born, you were destined to spread this message."

Connor turned again to see if Alexandra was being remotely controlled. "Beginning today, you will deliver this prophecy to the world."

"My God, Connor. Are you okay?" Danielle's voice echoed in Connor's ears.

"What happened? Where am I?" he answered.

"You hit your head on the car door. You were helping me change the oil before we went to the fair. You raised up and "bam!" I thought you were lying there dead for the last three minutes!"

"I'm fine, Danielle. I'm fine." As Daniel rubbed his head the vision of Alexandra played in his brain.

"I think I'll drive. You look a little white," Danielle continued. "I'm going inside to get my keys. Make sure you have enough coins for parking."

Connor dug a palm into his pocket. There were no coins but just a piece of blue cardboard reading *Orange County Fair* at the top. Connor flipped the card over and a freezing chill traced his spine when he read the words-

"Dearest Connor, The awesome thing about every day is you create it- Amazing Alexandra."

The Birthday Party

After Alandra staged a big birthday party for Dawson Winston when he turned 30, Dawson figured the next party wouldn't be as extravagant. Little Chef Burgers, after all, was the place they met when she worked as a table server. Dawson never forgot how she spilled the giant thirsty-sized Fruitola in his lap when she served it to his table. He supposed a difficult customer would have filed a lawsuit, claiming the thick blueberry-pineapple concoction permanently froze his testicles. The only thing that froze was time itself, and Dawson realized the big brown eyes and long, dark hair of a beautiful Guatemalan girl. Alandra grabbed a nearby towel, then paused right before she reached towards his lap. They both laughed, and so began a romance that led to marriage a year later.

Little Chef Burgers had quality beef greasers, and would remain their favorite fast-food joint long after Alandra quit her job. The seats were always soft and cushiony. The table servers were always friendly, and quick to bring delicious after-dinner snack mints in a tiny blue paper cup.

Dawson supposed nothing ever stayed the same, and Little Chef was certainly noisier than when he first met Alandra two years ago. They must have advertised heavily, because the cozy dining area of 1990 turned into individual hectic rooms with table servers running around everywhere with Fruitolas.

Of course business success doesn't always equal positive results. The noise level seemed to have doubled. Little Chef must have installed high-tech potato friers because an alarm went off every minute, sounding three obnoxious beeps right into his ear. An intercom sounded, "Key personnel to Room Three." Apparently, the management implemented mandatory training for all table servers, perhaps teaching them how to balance a tray of Fruitolas with one hand. Personal hand-held call buttons were conveniently added to each table if a customer needed immediate assistance.

Colorful lights blinked everywhere, and it was fun imagining that Little Chef was attempting to intensify the experience of his 32nd birthday. Before he had the chance to push the call button, a table server came to the other side of their table and asked if he wanted a refill. When he nodded, the server had a frothy drink ready with a fresh straw and a blue paper cup with a tiny white mint. With Dawson's hands by his side, the table server lifted the refreshing liquid to his lips and gently placed the mint on his tongue. Little Chef always made its patrons feel like royalty.

"Feel any older, birthday boy?" A flirtatious table server with a name tag spelling Alice awarded Dawson a single-candled cupcake bearing a warm blue-yellow flame. He thought thirty-two candles would have set off the fire sprinklers. Her lipstick and fingernails were bright red, which could have meant only one thing

– this girl was available.

"I love you, Dawson Winston," he heard Alandra whisper as she squeezed his hand. Alandra was always so emotional and cried at weddings of people she didn't even know. He hoped she was not becoming jealous of all the attention he was getting from the table servers. Her birthday card was folded upright on their table, and he knew it contained a long, mushy poem.

"Key personnel to Room Four," the intercom blared. He supposed that was their room because several table servers and a manager rushed in to make sure their dining experience was pleasant. The manager's light blue uniform made him almost disappear into the cold, blue walls. The manager reached over and adjusted a device that beeped with the same sound of the potato frier. Several tentacle-like cords branched out from the awkward contraption and were attached to Dawson's chest. Alice pushed another button and the back of his chair began to lower until it was completely flat.

There were three final beeps. The room became silent and dark. Dawson felt total peace and comfort as a warm blanket was tenderly placed over him.

"He's gone, Mrs. Winston," the nurse said as she turned the heart machine off. "I know he really enjoyed his 90th birthday."

They say ones hearing is the last thing to go before death, and Dawson distinctly heard Alandra's sweet voice as she kissed his forehead and whispered into his ear, "Goodbye, Dawson."

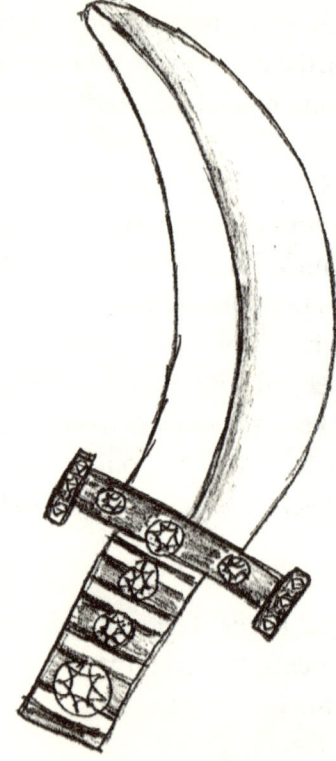

Shykor's Diamond

Shykor drew his golden sword from his sheath and stabbed it into the sky. The bright sun reflected a beam of yellow from the polished plastic. The handle was encrusted with crystal rhinestones, but looked like ocean blue sapphires and pigeon blood rubies set in a platinum halo.

Around Shykor's neck hung the Giant Flawless, which he pretended was the largest diamond in the land of Newport Beach. The Giant Flawless was surrounded by white diamonds and was cut so perfectly it was able to rip apart the sun's light and blind his enemies with all the colors of the rainbow. Shykor did not consider himself a warrior, but a messenger of wealth and abundance. He was armed with riches and was prepared to share with others. Shykor decided to give one diamond from his belt to any peasant who asked. He would not, however, give any gemstone to anyone who greedily wanted more than one.

Shykor saw Martina Wiggins run towards his empire, which was the third house on Seagull Street.

"My name is Shykor. Who goes there, peasant?" Shykor yelled.

"Excuse me? I thought your name was Michael. Peasant?" Martina said. "And isn't that what you wore for Halloween?"

"Today I am Shykor."

"Very nice name, Shykor. Wanna play house?"

Shykor liked Martina because she was the only girl on Seagull Street that liked to climb trees. Martina also had a girly side, and the last time they played house, Shykor had to kiss her after pretending he was coming home from work.

"How about you can be my assistant?" Shykor asked, hoping to get out of playing anything romantic.

"Sure," Martina said with excited eyes. "I love you, Shykor."

How was a mighty marvel of the universe supposed to respond? Shykor wondered. "Thank you, my lady," Shykor replied. Shykor loved to play with Martina, and he fondly remembered when she took all his money in the game called Cash. Shykor went bankrupt after only three die tosses.

"Am I like your queen?" Martina asked.

"Er, I suppose so. And here is a token of my gratitude, my lady." Shykor plucked a small rhinestone from his belt and handed it to Martina.

"It's so small," Martina complained.

"It may be small, but it is a beautiful diamond. Wear it and you will have great powers." Shykor tried to add value to the plastic stone.

"I want that one," Martina pointed to the largest crystal hanging on Shykor's neck.

"That is the Giant Flawless. It is the most precious diamond of the land," Shykor replied.

"I like it. It's really sparkly. I want that one. "

"That one is mine," Shykor said. "I must wear it to show that I'm the leader of the kingdom."

"But I am your queen," Martina insisted. "The peasants will know you are the leader if they see me wear it."

Martina was good with words and always seemed to get her way every time she came over to play.

"If you really love me, you should give it to me," Martina said.

Shykor gazed into Martina's eyes. She batted her eyes flirtatiously, exactly the same way as when Shykor had to give her over $10,000 in purple Cash tokens. He lifted the large white crystal talisman from his head and draped it over Martina.

"Oh, thank you, Shykor," Martina exclaimed. Then she leaned over and kissed him right on the lips.

Shykor wiped his mouth with his sleeve after Martina turned her head. He was not expecting to relinquish his most prized possession, but the glow in Martina's eyes could only be compared to the brilliant reflection of the Giant Flawless. He still had his rhinestone sword and his belt of precious crystals, he thought.

"Are we friends forever, Shykor?" Martina asked as she sat like the Queen of California.

After ten years had passed, Shykor realized he had made the best trade of his life. Although he had given Martina the largest gemstone in his treasure, Martina had given him something far more valuable, and that was her friendship.

The Neon 3

The sun had fallen. Stars had not quite sprinkled the sky. The old man fought his way to the door of the corner market amidst impatient cars dodging into empty parking stalls. Inside the market, tiny-wheeled grocery carts manned by grumpy shoppers whizzed everywhere without traffic regulations. One shopper bumped the man's cart while another complained nearby about the thickly-sliced bologna.

The old man quickly finished his shopping and propelled his cart toward checkout line number 3. The mesmerizing neon glow of the sign stopped him. It wasn't the shape or size of the 3 that made him pause, but the beautiful illumination! It was not just hot pink, but contained a hint of blue, making the intense color veer toward magenta. It must have been an illusion, but the 3 seemed to proudly float in front of its black square background.

The old man grasped the handle of the cart but an invisible force prevented him from moving it. He was always paralyzed in awe from any color one might consider even slightly purplish. As the old man continued gazing at the 3, the noise of the late-evening scramblers was silenced. The 3 became like the beacon of a lighthouse, inviting weary travelers to the paradise of its peaceful shore.

"Sir, would you like to go ahead of me?" A lady next to him politely interrupted his trance. She must have noticed the old man's cart contained only a few items. He nodded no thanks and let her swivel into the line.

Maybe it was the nature of being a Pisces, but he always became entranced when perceiving an object of wonder. A tiny leaf, a bejeweled insect, and now a 3 whose vibrant color burst through the dimmest aisle of a dank food market. The 3 made everything alive and real.

"Mister, are you okay?" The old man nodded to another lady in line, knowing by her glare she considered him to be insane. He wondered if anyone even noticed the exalting color. He returned his attention to the 3. The resplendent 3! The number seemed to pulse with a blinding luminescence. It summoned all to pause and be thankful for this Gift of Life. It split the darkness with hope. Like a supernova in a faraway galaxy, the 3 had the power to halt time. 3! The beautiful 3!...

"We are closing in five minutes, sir." The old man turned around to the deeper voice of a security guard. "Please get in line if you want to check out."

The old man obeyed by slowly wheeling his cart into the line. "Will that be cash or debit?" the attendant asked as she flipped off the lighted sign. The unpleasant noise of impatient shoppers poured back into reality as the 3 was blackened. The man paid and was ushered out the door. Although he was not religious, he later testified how he discovered God, who broke through this dimension, disguised as a neon number.

No Dream is Impossible

"What do you mean, you *can't* do it?" Laslo Laporo asked the small-framed Vietnamese programmer.

After five hours of tinkering at the jewelry store's master computer, Lan Dong finally admitted it would be impossible to make Laslo's demands come true.

"This may take thirty to forty more hours of programming. I think I will be able to locate four percent of males ages 20 to 40 that have just arrived at or left a restaurant, a bar, or a religious establishment. But there is no way I can tell if they are in a relationship, want to get married, or want to buy an engagement ring."

Laslo peeked up from the diamond he was appraising. A perfectly-cut diamond gleamed brilliantly in his tweezers. Paying $450 per hour was pocket change, he always thought, if a computer genius could make his store a more efficient diamond trading company. It was against the rules, however, for any paid worker to claim anything was impossible.

"Thank you, Mr. Dong, for your services. Here is your check for five hours rendered. Have a nice day." There was no sense in

getting angry. It was indeed a far-fetched dream. Maybe it was an-
thropological, but Laslo knew that a man in love could decide at
any moment to invest his entire yearly salary on the woman of his
desires. Laslo's diamonds came with strict grading, free lifetime
inspection, and low prices that no other dealer could match. His
dream was to notify every man who was searching for this precious stone that would symbolize a lifetime relationship.

Laslo was passionate about his business. He knew a man in
love was impulsive and elusive. At any moment, a man could be
spellbound by Cupid's invisible arrow, summoned to the nearest
jewelry store, and pour out his hard-earned money onto a granite
sales counter. He understood how the modern world attempted to
turn beautiful diamonds into bland commodities, and offered them
on every street corner including department stores and television
shopping channels. The joke in the business was that diamonds
would soon be sold in grocery stores. He knew that a man would
make his final choice from a sad list of resources, and be left feeling empty. If he only had the right connections, he would possess
a gem that would contain a tiny piece of the diamond merchant's
heart that sold the gem to him.

He was tired of men complaining that they paid too much at
their corner jewelry store, or being misinformed about the quality, or that the stone fell out, or chipped, or cracked. To Laslo, a
diamond was far more than a precious gem, but an eternal symbol
of a man's love. Laslo never bothered with what others thought
of him, but if a man ever invested in the king of all gems, *born
from the earth and reborn on a woman*, he wanted it to be from
his collection of beautiful diamonds.

Orville Klingster from NDii, Inc. arrived ten minutes early

the following morning. Orville was a self-proclaimed computer genius that sold himself well over the telephone, and whose voice resonated with confidence and charisma. His appearance, on the other hand, did not match his voice. Orville was huge, out-of-shape, and slow moving. At least he wore a tie, but the knot was overly thick and drawn tight around his collar.

"Good morning, Mr. Laslo Laporo."

"You know our mission, correct?" Laslo replied.

"Yes. I will not charge you extra because I arrived early. I will accomplish your dream. Please authorize this standard form saying I will be paid $950 for each hour worked. As I explained on the phone, I will need a retainer of my minimum charge of $10,000 to begin."

Laslo admired confidence and had not witnessed it in such a long time. He believed anything could be accomplished, no matter one's appearance, simply with good intentions and unshakable belief.

"Can I have that?" Orville pointed at the hungry-sized Choco-Cream in the customer candy dish.

"Be our guest, Mr. Klingster."

"Show me the computer with the master files," Orville said before he finished swallowing. "What is your administrative password?"

Even the key personnel did not know the master password that also commanded the current wholesale prices of polished diamonds in Tel Aviv and Belgium. He knew that when Orville left, he would have to devise another secret word. Laslo looked over each of his shoulders then wrote "FlyUp" in tiny letters on a piece of scrap paper and slid it towards Orville.

"Before we begin, Laslo, may I make a suggestion?" Laslo nodded. "If you want to sell your diamonds, why don't you just advertise in wedding magazines?"

"Mr. Klingster," Laslo began firmly. "I did not hire you as a marketing consultant. Please complete your mission."

Orville shrugged while crumbling the chocolate wrapper. "Oh, well. They say diamonds are forever."

"Yeah, death and taxes are also forever," Laslo replied. Orville cracked his large knuckles and began plinking at the keypad.

Laslo was hardly ever diplomatic when sharing marketing ideas with others. He had began his career at seventeen, at a time when a young man had only one design option for his fiancé's engagement ring: a single diamond set in four prongs.

He considered jewelers who advertised in bridal magazines ones who threw their money in the trash. The same went for those who advertised in media that sold wedding cakes, wedding dresses, and Hawaiian honeymoon vacations. The dilemma was that by the time a girl was dreaming of these accessories, it was too late, for she already had the diamond on her finger. The rock came first, the limousine ride came second.

"Was anyone going to eat the other ChocoCream?" Orville asked. Laslo reached over and tossed the large brick of candy to Orville. "Thanks. They say sugar is food for the brain." Orville peeled the foil wrapping like a banana and took a large bite."

While Orville painfully pecked one key at a time, Laslo admired a three-carat diamond under the Spectra Light. The proportions were perfect, and the gem shone with colors constrained deep inside its crystallized carbon walls. The stone breathed life into any observer, and was a hard-to-find treasure. Through the barrage of mass advertising, it would be difficult for a man to discover a gem like this. He would be mesmerized by another stores fancy guarantees or puffed appraisals. He may even be lured to take the gem home, and make high interest installments for the rest of his life.

An hour passed. From the angle Laslo was sitting, it appeared Orville was sleeping. His head was lowered and his hands were relaxed on each side of the keypad. One hand still held the empty remains of a metallic purple candy wrapper. Either he was daydreaming into the computer screen or he fell into a chocolate coma.

"Wake up, Mr. Klingster!" Laslo screamed from his desk.

Startled, Orville sat erect. "Hey, I wasn't sleeping!" Orville snapped back. "Do you want to give me a heart attack? I am programming, and when I'm programming I need to think."

"Okay," Laslo said. "I just wanted to make sure you didn't die. I don't offer life insurance."

Two more hours passed, and Laslo did not remember Orville tapping more than a dozen keystrokes. Then he saw Orville lift his huge finger into the air and dive in slow motion with a final stab into the middle of the keypad. "I am finished!" Orville exclaimed loudly as he sat upright with a grin.

Startled, Laslo almost dropped a new shipment of diamonds onto the floor. "Finished with what, Mr. Klingster?"

"I think I have what you want, Laslo."

"For God's sake, Mr. Klingster. Please tell me what you have."

"When you press this button, it will show a list of approximately 1,000 men in your area who are in love, men who are beginning to get that tickle in their stomachs right before they pop the question, right before they pull the trigger."

"And how do you know that?" Laslo asked with anticipation.

Men who are newly in love hold an image of their loved one in their minds for several minutes at a time, and often throughout the day and night. When a man is in love, he constantly daydreams of his lover, and sees her in every car that passes, in every picture he admires, and hears her in every song on the radio. There are also measurable endorphins that are associated with this mental imaging. The new technology of EMI, or endorphin-mental imaging, can now be detected through new cell-phone technology. Activating this computer script will give you a list of these men's emails and telephone numbers. It may not be one hundred percent accurate, because stress or anxiety may skew the results."

"Very interesting," Laslo rubbed his chin.

"I'm a genius, Laslo. That's why my fee is high. You will now be able to get real-time love vibrations from every man who holds a cell phone to his ear. Pressing the second button will send an email, making them aware of your engagement ring services."

"Press the button now!" Laslo commanded from his desk.

"Are you sure you don't want to do a test first?" asked Orville.

"What's the worst can happen?" asked Laslo. "...save another poor soul from going to Jimmy's Jewelers?"

Orville clicked the purple icon on the computer screen. Within two minutes, all the lights blinked on the company telephone lines.

"We have a diamond order, Laslo," an assistant said. "He wants to know how soon you can send him a two-carat diamond mounted in your signature-designed 14-karat engagement ring."

"You are a genius, Mr. Klingster," said Laslo, as he gazed at Orville's business card. Can I ask what NDii stands for?"

"Sure, Laslo. It stands for *No Dream is Impossible*."

hyperbolic family $\sum_{k=1}^{n=2} k^2$

recall $\cos\theta$, $\sin\theta$

basic

$1 = \sin^2\theta + \cos^2\theta$

new family of functions

sin hyperbolic. $\sinh x = \dfrac{e^x - e^{-x}}{2}$

$\cosh x = \dfrac{e^x + e^{-x}}{2}$

tanh x
$\dfrac{\pi}{2}$
$-\dfrac{\pi}{2}$

$\displaystyle\int_0^{\frac{\pi}{2}} \dfrac{1}{x^2 + q^2}\, dx$

Let $u = x^2$

$du = 2x\, dx$

Top secret

Illustrated by Michaela Watson.

The Secret of Zero

Everybody laughed at Carl Bickles as Mr. Rogers was teaching everyone about space. The fourth grade class was filled with cool artifacts, including a large wooden dinosaur on Mr. Rogers' desk. Marcus Wilson was always fascinated how the Brontosaurus trampled heavily upon the earth. He was saddened about their demise when Mr. Rogers said the Ice Age froze their blood like lizards in a snowstorm.

Carl always asked stupid questions. When Mr. Rogers explained how it was impossible to fly a rocket to the sun because of the unbearable heat, Carl raised his hand with a solution. "Why can't we just go at night?" The class giggled. Even Marcus knew that there was no such thing as day or night when it came to the sun. It was Earth that revolved... or was it *rotated*? He always got the two mixed up.

Time for the math lesson. Marcus looked up and saw a handsome picture of Columbus on the wall. He always daydreamed he would be like him. A man whose only mission was to prove to his family and friends that Earth was round. He was an explorer and a hero. Marcus' mission, however, was to discover a new planet. As he became older, everyone would probably fly spaceships, but he was going to be known as the first person to land on Saturn.

"Twelve plus twelve equals twenty-four!" Mr. Rogers spoke louder to wake Marcus from his slumber. "And no matter how many zeros you add together, the answer is still zero."

Impossible, Marcus thought. If someone added enough zeros together it would have to make a positive number. He raised his hand. "Mr. Rogers, if you added enough zeros together, wouldn't that have to equal something?"

The classroom became silent. Mildred chuckled. Carl Bickles pondered the possibility. Mr. Rogers paused for a second, gave a slight smirk, and replied, "No, Marcus, I don't think that is correct. Zero plus zero is always zero, no matter how many you add."

Marcus' theory was shunned. He thought even scientists made mistakes. Yeah, maybe a hundred or even a thousand zeros would still equal zero. But what about adding ten thousand hundred magillion zeros? Has anyone ever tried that? One of these days the world will know. Maybe it will be only the tiniest fraction, but Marcus knew it would add to something. Mark his words. "Marcus Wilson discovers the Secret of Zero – Baffles World."

Opposites

What is big? What is small?
Is there a difference between tiny and tall?
(Even a bug on a stalk of grass
Is huge when viewed through a lens of thick glass)

What is up? What is down
as I point to a star as the earth spins around?
When is young old? When is day night?
When is cold hot and black becomes white?

Sweet or sour, happy or sad
Inside, outside, sane or mad
Helping, hurting, peace or war
When should a whisper become a roar?

Angels, devils, heaven or hell
Are they real or imagined? Are we under a spell?
Destroy or create? Should I break or mend?
Is everything nothing, is the beginning the end?

When am I born, alive, or dead?
I ponder this thought as I rise from my bed
When I'm awake, is it just a dream?
Are things I think real not what they seem?

When I die is it really the end?
Or simply a chance to start over again?

To make sense of this world, my ignorance I hide
Vibrations of Love I rudely divide
Beautiful or ugly, I always decide
A bug is a butterfly if I am perfect-eyed

I surrender the myths of all I've been taught
Inventing illusions on this tiny, blue dot
We have created our world from the sum of our thoughts

The Elevator

"They pay for parking if you save your receipt," said the lady slumped next to Jon Baskerville in the juror assembly room. The lady wore a floppy blouse with a large clamp-on tag saying 124 California.

"Yeah, thank you. I have my ticket in my pocket for validation," Jon replied. "What happens next?"

"You get one of these beauties," the lady pointed at her official jurors badge, now almost hanging sideways from her top.

"Very fashionable," Jon jested as he checked his cell phone for the time.

"My name's Lonna," the lady said with an outstretched hand.

"I'm Jon. I'm not sure how I got here. My wife said the jury summons that came in the mail looked pretty official. You know, the kind that makes you feel like if you don't come they will throw you in jail."

"Do you always dress in a pin-striped suit this early?" asked Lonna.

"Yes, my job requires that I'm dressed a notch better than my clients. I guess it makes them feel like I know what I'm doing."

"What do you do?"

"When a city builds a new skyscraper, they need something that transports people to each floor. That's where my company comes in." Jon scribbled a weird formula on a small notepad and slid it back into his vest.

"So you build stairways?"

"No," Jon laughed. "We sell elevators. Why do you think America is overweight? The average person avoids lifting even one foot if they can prevent it. People love to simply press a button and be transported somewhere else. It makes them feel powerful and invincible."

"Interesting." Lonna leaned closer.

"Are you familiar with the 'Door Close' button?"

"Of course," Lonna answered. "You press it and the door closes quicker.

"No, it doesn't. Did you know that button hasn't been functional since the 1990's? It simply creates the illusion of personal control. The same goes for crosswalk buttons and many office thermostats. No matter how many times that button is depressed, the door will only close when it thinks every passenger has entered safely. As it shuts, the person who pressed the button will experience the placebo of perceived power."

"I bet you make a lot of money," Lonna interrupted.

"The salespeople do, that's for sure," Jon began. "I'm the software guy who makes sure the elevator does not go to the fifteenth floor and the third floor at the same time."

"That would be impossible," said Lonna.

"Maybe, but don't think it wouldn't try. An elevator has a brain, just like a human. It has to always make split second decisions. When several people press a bunch of buttons at the same time, the elevator has to know where to go first. For example, what if you are on the first floor and someone presses 16 and another presses 2? The elevator has to know to drop off the second floor passenger before rising to the sixteenth floor."

"Very interesting," said Lonna, as she straightened her badge. "Be prepared for an all day adventure, Jon. You may be sitting here for hours. Hope you don't have a meeting today, but being a juror is very noble. The last time I was here a husband beat his wife to a pulp. We all knew he was guilty, and I was happy knowing justice was served."

Jon had so many thoughts in his head, he hardly heard Lonna. "And what if someone hops on the third floor and wants to go to the fifth? Should the elevator drop off the passenger at the fifth or should it ride the passenger all the way to the highest floor already pressed? I'm telling you, Lonna, sometimes an elevator gets frustrated just like a person."

"Of the people, by the people, for the people. You can make a difference!" the intercom blared. A giant white screen slowly unfolded from the ceiling showing the American flag flapping in the breeze. *"A trial by jury is what makes our nation strong. Now is your chance to weigh the evidence that will be presented so justice can be served."*

"So, how's business?" Lonna immediately knew she should have mentioned the weather instead, for Jon was ready to answer.

"Sometimes we make money, sometimes we lose money," Jon began. "But you can't believe all the things that can go wrong, like if there is a fire or the electricity goes out, or if the elevator gets stuck between floors, or if the software has a glitch. People also want to get to the bottom floor quickly but they would prefer not crashing. I haven't got all the bugs worked out, but we are starting to upgrade the software for our former clients."

"Justice must be served." the projector screen showed a judge slamming his gavel.

"I heard our lunch recess is at 12:30," Lonna tried to change the subject.

"The software has to work flawlessly. One crazy woman sued us just because she was stuck in the dark for twenty minutes. She claimed she had claustrophobia and now has a permanent fear of all elevators. The bug I'm trying to fix is the very small chance the driveshaft cord could become compromised if someone accidentally pressed two buttons simultaneously. And then again, there's always that one fool passenger who plays bellboy, asks everyone which floor they want, and presses buttons like crazy."

"Sounds dangerous."

"True, but life is dangerous, right? What are the real chances that you are going to be hit by a bus? What are the odds that a meteor will come crashing down on your house?" Jon fetched his notepad and added a few symbols to his last formula.

"Mike Anderson, Jeremy Monas, Jon Baskerville, come to Window Four for your juror badges," an older man announced into the microphone.

"There's my cue. Good luck to you," Jon said to Lonna as he rose and straightened his tie.

An older woman with no expression and a monotone voice greeted Jon at the window, "Here's your badge. Go to room number twenty-one on the sixth floor."

Jon shuffled through the crowd of possible jurors into the hallway. He dreamed about his bonus if he closed his last deal. Of course life always come with obstacles, and he worried about the new software upgrades that were being installed in the older buildings. His new software was intelligent but there was always room for improvement. Still, he knew that several of the updated elevators were becoming finicky when too many buttons were pressed at the same time.

A great rumble rocked the building. "Earthquake!" several startled bystanders yelled.

"This is the big one!" A heckler shouted from the end of the hallway. The oversized hanging photo of the first county judge broke onto the granite floor. The plant by the water fountain collapsed.

The door of the lobby elevator opened and revealed four passengers slumped over each other and moaning.

'Dear God,' Jon thought. 'Someone must have pressed two buttons at exactly the same time.'

"You can make a difference!" The intercom continued to boom from the assembly room.

"Justice must be served."

Madam Sophie

Madam Sophie lit the incense sticks in the mind reading room and dimmed the lights once again. "Next, please," she spoke through the black curtains to her final customer in the waiting room. A young lady with curly brown hair shuffled through the thick, dark cloth and aromatic smoke. "Please sit," she commanded to the lady. "Each question is one hundred dollars."

The lady already had a hundred dollar bill clinched in her sweaty palm. "And what question do you have for me this evening?" Madam Sophie asked.

The lady handed the wet bill to the madam. "Did he forgive me?"

"Did who forgive you?" Madam Sophie was always the one who asked the most questions. After all, how can you help a customer if one does not know all the facts?

"My husband. Did he forgive me before he left?"

"Yes.. your husband," the madam began as she gazed into the crystal ball on the table. "Uh, yes…he seemed quite upset." Madam Sophie was always her sharpest in the beginning of the day. In the nighttime, however, she was exhausted and ready to go home. "Yes…I see him," she began, wiggling her fingers above the crystal ball. "Did he have darkish hair?"

"No, it was blond and sandy," the lady answered.

Madam Sophie slowly nodded her head in agreement. She paused, scrunched the wrinkles on her forehead with concern and replied, "Yes…that's correct. I see him. Would you say he had sandyish blonde hair?"

"Yes! That's him!" The lady cried with relief.

Madam Sophie was skilled in the art of persuasion and psychology. Nevertheless, she was tired from the day and wanted to make her last appointment brief. "Your husband wants you to be with him. He said he loves you and forgives you and wants you to go back to him now."

The lady's face grew sad. "I didn't mean to kill him."

"What!?" Madam Sophie's eyes widened with surprise.

"He told me several times to turn off the main electricity valve

while he was rewiring the house. I thought I did. Maybe I turned
it the wrong way. Maybe I turned it off and on again. I know he's
upset but I'm glad he still loves me. Thank you, Madam Sophie."
The lady got up from her chair and headed out of the curtains
toward the front door.

"Wait!" Madam Sophie called. "Where are you going?"

"To be with Eric like you told me to. There's no reason for me
to live anymore."

"I didn't know he was dead!" Madam Sophie frantically
waved her fingers over the crystal. "Sometimes this crystal ball
gives confusing signals."

"Thank you so much, Madam Sophie," the lady said, showing
her fist sign of joy. "He wants to be with me. That's all I needed to
know."

The loud shot that followed a few seconds later did not need
an explanation. Madam Sophie ran to the front door where the
neon green crystal ball blinked by the entrance of her boutique.
On the steps below was the lady, folded in a peculiar way. A pistol
was inches from her hand. As blood oozed from her head onto the
brick pavement, a peaceful smile seemed to be frozen on her lips.

Where Does a Tree Begin?

Where does a tree begin?
Does it start at the top?
Or could that be the end?

Perhaps it's the leaf
That drinks the sun
But if there were no light
The tree would be none

Branches twist out
With dangling limbs
But I still do not know
Where a tree begins

Is it the trunk
That cuddles the ground?
Or is there more tree
That's much further down?

The roots snarl deep
Into the dirt
Is that where we'll find
The tree's secret birth?

Searching for water
They twist and coil
And sip the moisture
From rich, dark soil

But still not the beginning
Of the mystery tree
Because without earth
The tree would not be

Perhaps trees have
No beginning or end
Or boundary to hold
Our perceptions within

If this is true
Where do we fit in?
So it is now I must ask
Where do *we* begin?

The Devil's Doom Roller Coaster

The Devil's Doom roller coaster thundered across the steel rails just above their heads.

"So long, suckers!" Nora yelled to the people waiting in line from her confined cockpit of Sector 4. Her breasts always looked larger from being squished together from the tight-fitting shoulder harness of the death-defying thrill ride. "Catch you in another lifetime!"

Nora and Jovan had been married for almost three years, and she made Jovan promise their lives would be filled with adventure. Jovan preferred picnics, miniature golf, and an occasional show. Nora enjoyed only one thing in life-- being slung around mercilessly on Devil's Doom. She would make Jovan pay ten times extra for the metal Ride-It-Again passes that hung around their necks. The key-like passes would let them jump to the front of the line and ride three times in a row without getting out of their seats. Jovan pulled the harness down as it clicked tight against his chest. He smelled vomit from a kid who couldn't handle the last ride.

"Isn't this fun, Jovan?" Nora always squeaked as they

plopped into a coaster car. "Can we do this for the rest of our lives?"

"Can we do something else for a change?" Jovan yelled even though she was sitting next to him. This would be the twelfth time they had rode the metal beast today, and his head was sore from being whacked around from the sharp twists.

"No, Jovan. I want us to do this forever."

Jovan looked by Nora's seat and noticed the main screw of her harness was loose. After riding the coaster hundreds of times, he was familiar with every piece that held the contraption together. The workers ran by each side of the coaster, shoving down everyone's harness to lock it in place. The tram began eerily creaking across the runway. "See you on the other side of hell!" Nora yelled at the patrons waiting for the next set of cars.

Jovan wanted to say something about the loose screw, but his mouth was frozen. Not in fear, but because Nora would call him a baby or a worrywart. He dreamed of the coaster in his sleep. One big drop, two tight loops, one large loop, then a sharp turn that would shake one's brains out and make you feel like you were going to fly through the air.

The coaster crawled slowly into the sky. The passengers began screaming before it reached the drop off. The riders in the front already waved their arms in the air. The nut jiggled as the coaster climber higher. Surely the safety crew checked each car after every ride. Or maybe they didn't. Devil's Doom was the most popular ride at Thrill-Adventure. Who had time to check every car after every ride?

"Oh, Jovan, aren't you glad we can do this every day?" Jovan didn't answer Nora's question. "Hang on, Jovan."

Jovan reached over to see if was his imagination or if the screw was really loose. He lodged his Ride-It-Again pass into the grooves of the bolt and cranked it with all his might. He accidentally loosened instead of tightened it. The bolt spun half a revolution. The coaster descended down the first and steepest drop. As the coaster pulled back up for a two-second pause he reached over again with the metal talisman and turned the screw another revolution. The vertigo from the drop must have made him confused because he turned it the same direction. The bolt began to dangle from its socket.

The coaster twirled its two tight loops. After the pause, the coaster entered the giant loop.

"AHHHH!" The riders always screamed the same pitch when falling into the vortex of death, as Nora called it. Jovan reached over and gave the screw a final spin, again in the wrong direction, and the nut twisted off and fell to earth.

"What are you doing?" Nora turned to look at him.

"Just making sure you're safe!" he screamed. What else could he say?

The coaster entered the head-bending twist. The one that makes one take three aspirins after getting off the ride. The one that would break ones neck if it were not attached properly. The turn that would send one flying to the moon if the shoulder harness was not properly secured.

Then, in slow motion, Jovan saw Nora's harness lift over her head and her body ascend out of her seat. He did not know who screamed louder, the other riders or Nora.

"AHHhhhhhhhh....," Nora's voice began loudly then quickly faded as the coaster ended its writhing turn.

The rest of the day was ruined for the thrill seekers of Devil's Doom. The ride braked at the landing and the workers ushered everyone out. Security asked Jovan questions for three and a half hours before they let him go.

May the reader not think badly of Jovan. He did what he thought was best. He had good intentions.

He really did.

Apathy

After school, Kayla Kim cleaned her aquarium. She filled
a small glass jar with water, and carefully transported each fish
into their temporary home. It was a fantastic scenery—two dozen
multi-colored fish swarming tightly in a few ounces of water.
Rather than continuing to scrub the tank, Kayla marveled at her
new creation. The fish splashed their vivid colors back and forth
like a most beautiful painting. The neons darted up and down, the
zebras swirled like a wild tornado, and the beta even flared his
blue fins.

Kayla had to share her experience. She bounced into the kitch-
en and displayed the colorful motion picture to her parents and
their company. Everyone was talking and no one seemed to care
about her fish. Her father said nothing. Her company said nothing.
Her mother finally responded, "Yes, that's pretty." Everyone saw
'fish in a jar.' Kayla saw an aquatic masterpiece.

As she carefully cradled the jar in her hands, the afternoon
sun poured through the glass and reflected bright beams of red,
gold and green from the metallic scales of the small sea creatures.
The jar contained the secrets of the universe. It was an unwritten
poem about the meaning of life. For that one brief moment, Kayla
actually held the origin of the cosmos in her arms. The tiny jar of

fish and water encompassed the miniature world of all knowledge, wonder, and imagination.

Kayla put the thermostat from the aquarium into the jar so the fish would not get cold and went to the store to buy milk and bread for mom. When she returned the water had gotten way too hot. All of the fish were floating on top.

And nobody saw the beauty she saw.

Nobody cared.

Kayla always remembered holding the universe in her hands. Although difficult to understand, she gradually learned that any experience was not the same for everyone. Two persons could never share the same pair of eyes, and others do not always understand the joy we try to share.

The important thing is that she was aware of that beautiful slice of time, and that is all that mattered.

Kayla flushed the flaccid fish down the toilet.

A Tourmaline for Irmaleen

A one-carat diamond dangled below the watermelon tour-maline at the jewelry store. "I've always wanted one of those," Irmaleen Crawford said to her husband of fifty years.

"Why in the world would you want that?" Ernie asked, who was upbeat and jolly for a man in his late seventies.

"I saw one in a magazine and liked it. You know pink and green are my favorite colors. You do remember that, don't you, Ernie?" Irmaleen batted her eyes flirtatiously. Ernie tried to appear tough, but the frail man couldn't hide his good-natured demeanor behind his happy wrinkles. The big half-century anniversary was coming up in a week, and Irmaleen loved all things sparkly.

"What about a cubic zirconia? Don't they look the same?" Ernie said.

"Be quiet, Ernie. I'm sure Alex does not have fake jewelry in his store."

"Fake?" Ernie exclaimed. "I'm talking about real cubic zirconia." Alex Andrews always loved the interactions between

couples in love, but it was a joy to watch two elderly lovebirds
playing together like children.

Irmaleen stared at Ernie, paused, and nodded her head for the
final cue to make the decision. Alex was positive that this commu-
nication had taken place hundreds of times during their marriage,
and Ernie probably yielded to Irmaleen each time.

"Let's see what it looks like," Ernie began. "Alex, can you
throw that bauble around Irmaleen's neck and please tell her it
looks too gaudy?" Ernie joked a lot, and probably kept Irmaleen
laughing since the day they were married.

"There ya go, Irmaleen," Alex said after he snapped the clasp
on the back of the small woman's neck. Alex turned the showcase
counter mirror to face Irmaleen. "What will your friends think
about the new Irmaleen?"

"Oh, Alex," Irmaleen began. "We don't have that many
friends coming around anymore at our age. I just want something
to enjoy so I can remember Ernie every time I look in the mirror."

"Oh brother," Ernie exclaimed. "Now she's pulling at the
heart strings, Alex."

"Can I have it?" Irmaleen nearly tripped onto the floor as she
quickly turned from the counter mirror to face Ernie.

"Be careful, Irmaleen! The doctor said you are not allowed to
get too excited about things."

The couples' faces turned more serious as Ernie put his arm

on Irmaleen's shoulder while she held her chest.

"Is she okay?" Alex asked.

"She has a problem with her heart, Alex," Ernie said with concern. Irmaleen froze briefly in her upright state, wondering if this would be her final moment.

"Whew, I'm better now," Irmaleen said as the pink returned to her cheeks.

"Are you sure you want it?" Ernie asked Irmaleen for confirmation.

"Yes." Irmaleen said confidently while fondling the gleaming diamond below the pink-green gemstone.

"Okay, Irmaleen, but that means we will have to forget about that trip to the North Pole you always wanted." Irmaleen was too overwhelmed to laugh, but still managed a chuckle from Ernie's one-liners.

"Hooray! A tourmaline for Irmaleen!" Ernie and Irmaleen both laughed. "We don't need a box, Alex. I'm sure she wants to wear it now. At our age, we just celebrate every day like it is our anniversary." Ernie handed his credit card to an associate at the sales counter. "This was a lot of fun, Alex, and thank you so much for the fifty percent off senior citizen discount."

"Oh be quiet, Ernie," Irmaleen interrupted. "Alex, Ernie was a born comedian. Now you know what I've had to live with for the past fifty years."

"You will receive so much enjoyment from your new necklace, Irmaleen. I do hope you will bring Ernie back to our store again soon," Alex said.

"Alex, you have been so wonderful to us," Irmaleen replied, then turned toward her husband. "Ernie, if anything ever happens to me, you must promise me that you will come back to Alex and set this diamond in a ring for yourself."

"Oh, Irmaleen, I don't think..." Ernie's smile diminished.

"I mean it, Ernie. Alex, I want to say this for you both to hear. I want you to set this diamond in a ring for Ernie when I am done with it."

"Okay, Irmaleen. I will do that, but I'm sure you will be enjoying this diamond for many, many years to come."

It wasn't every day that Alex got a hug from his customers, but Irmaleen embraced him with the love of a mother. "Thank you, Alex, for a wonderful experience. And thank you, Ernie, for my anniversary gift." Irmaleen squeezed her husband and kissed his cheek.

Four months later, Ernie returned to the jewelry boutique. "Hello, Alex," he said with sadness in his eyes as he tenderly placed his wife's necklace onto the counter.

"Hello Ernie. Is it time to give Irmaleen's necklace a good cleaning and polishing?" Alex instinctively knew what had happened, but hoped for the best as he tried to conceal the quiver from his throat.

"She didn't make it, Alex," Ernie began. "She died about two weeks after we took the necklace home. It took me three months to be able to return here."

"I'm so sorry, Ernie."

"That's alright, Alex. But she received so much pleasure in the short time she wore it. We joked every night about the tourmaline for Irmaleen."

"I'm happy to hear that, Ernie."

"Irmaleen made me promise to make a ring for myself with her diamond. I knew this was going to happen. I just didn't know it would be this soon. Nothing lasts forever, Alex, except for the wonderful memories of those who loved us. So, here I am. You sure made a good impression with Irmaleen. I suppose any other husband would have been a little jealous. But I have to say she really liked you, Alex, just as I do. I never dreamed that a jeweler would have ever been in my wife's will."

The diamond business was always the business of love, Alex Andrews thought, and he was always grateful for choosing the profession.

"It's time for me to move on, Alex. I'm healthy. I'm happy. This diamond will always remind me of the best fifty years of my life."

Alex carefully removed the diamond from its setting. "Let me check your finger size, Ernie."

The Falling Car

Zack Zimmerman supposed he was driving too fast while zooming left around a big turn on top of Black Mountain. It was a cold, moonless night, and the head beams illuminated only a few feet of the winding dirt road in front of the black Jeep.

He saw the turn approaching and cut his wheels to the left accordingly but there must have been a malfunction in the axle. It was as if he did not turn the wheel sharp enough. The car refused to stay on the bumpy road and wanted to take a wider angle. It happened all at once and in slow motion. The car seemed to take on a consciousness of its own, and with a daredevil instinct, gracefully catapulted up a smooth, sloped dirt mound into the sky fifteen feet away from the edge of the cliff.

Zack was airborne in the flying car. The vehicle did not tumble, but remained in an upright position like an airplane. It must have been a dream, for anyone else would have screamed, or said a silent prayer, or rapidly played the movie of their life in their mind. He guessed he felt there was no need to worry about any of these things and that one cannot always choose his fate.

Although he could not even see his own hands, the automobile must have began a rapid descent into the dark abyss. The

engine was silent, and there was no whoosh of air, like a para-
chutist must hear as he descends from an airplane. The headlights
were useless, and were not able to cut through the thick blackness.
Although he could have been falling at the speed of light, he felt
motionless in the womb of the car. If this were indeed a dream, he
could alter his fate by simply opening the door and soar safely to
the ground with outstretched arms. Instead he froze in time, and
began a free fall as everything vanished.

Zack did not feel the G-force of gravity pull him towards the
ground. He could have imagined he was hovering motionless or
flying straight ahead instead of down. Several seconds passed.
Surely the car had reached terminal velocity. In considering the
downward speed and the closeness of the ground, he was sure the
great impact was near. Ground Zero was soon approaching. The
car was now a bomb and seconds away from detonation.

His wife, Mariah, and his two daughters flashed in his brain.
Perhaps it was for a millisecond, but it was long enough to for-
ward the scene where they played like kids on that street trolley
in San Francisco. Bella and Brianna hung from the sidebars like
it was a flying electric bus. He remembered the hilarious moment
when their little dog Buster got tangled in Mariah's freshly laun-
dered undergarments.

Zack could not tell if his eyes were opened or closed. The
only thing familiar was the wheel in his grasp, but he knew that
steering the car left or right would not change his destiny.

Then Zack felt his body slanting sharply to the side. The
heater was on high and his breathing became difficult. He felt
surrounded by an unknown consciousness. Surely he would have

hit bottom by now. Surely there was another cliff or tree branch to scrape against. Can one really fall from the top of a mountain to the bottom without colliding against a protruding rock? Is there such a thing as a straight drop from a mountain? Even a snow skier will tumble as he falls.

"Stop!" Zack screamed, slamming the brake pedal. He felt his seatbelt tug sharply at his shoulder.

"Zack, wake up," Mariah said, hovering above him. "It's Saturday! We better leave early if we want to drive to Black Mountain before dark."

What is Me?

Who am I? What is me?
Am I more than I can see?
Whom is this who returns my stare
From my mirrors misty glare?

Why am I here? What's my name?
Just let me know from where I came
Are these thoughts inside my head?
Or is there Something Else instead?

Is my life just someone's game?
I ask my twin inside this frame
A tiny voice spoke from within
That let me know where I have been

In humble awe, on tiles, I kneel
I touch my face, I must be real
In dreams I fall, and fly, and soar
But now I feel this ice cold floor

You are both human and divine
The universe you can define
Just look around and you will see
The (— —) you've left behind

Fill in the blank carefully.
This is you.

The Hairspray Can Explosion

Caution: Flammable. Contents under pressure.

Marcus Wilson eyeballed the label of his mom's used hairspray can.

Do not expose near fire or flame. May explode if temperature rises above 120 degrees. To an adult, this message is never read. To a twelve-year old aspiring scientist, however, this meant, *I am an awesome bomb*.

Marcus discovered the container sticking halfway out of the garbage can, so he was not really stealing anything. He toted the metal can down the hill and began to collect dry twigs and sticks for the ultimate hairspray can bonfire.

Fearing fallout or shooting debris, Marcus had to be shielded from harm. His dad's new truck was parked in the back driveway and Marcus determined it would provide adequate shelter from a terrifying explosion. Just before detonation, Marcus could escape into the shiny blue truck. The windows seemed thick enough to provide protection while also offering a great view. The glass tinting would also protect his eyes from a possible nuclear flash. As a scientist, Marcus needed to scribe detailed notes, so he ran into the house to retrieve his binder of secret formulas and inventions.

Marcus neatly constructed a pyramid of dried debris in the grass ten footsteps away from the truck, and scooted dead leaves inside. '*Laid can sideways on top of branches*,' Marcus scribbled in his binder. A match would not cause a large enough fire, he thought, and he would need something extra to create 120-degree flames.

Marcus galloped up the hill to the back porch and spotted the can of lighter fluid his dad stored by the grill. His mom never understood his passion for experiments but he knew one day he would discover an unknown secret that would revolutionize the world. Would the can just sizzle, with the remaining hairspray shooting out? Would it be projected into the air? Would it go sideways or spin around like a top? These were important questions that could change the future of hairspray can design. His parents did not let him use matches without supervision, but in the name of science, he hoped they would make an exception. Marcus stuffed the matches, fuel, and binder in his arms and raced back down the hill.

After a generous squirt of the liquid, Marcus scratched a match across its cardboard box. It flared but immediately blew out from a gust of wind. On the second strike, Marcus placed the burning stick inside the pyramid. The flames began to consume the dead leaves and the dark enclosure became illuminated.

Marcus ran away, hopped inside the truck and slammed the door. He grabbed his dad's oversized sunglasses from the dashboard for extra eye protection and flipped open his binder. 'Flames growing higher, can turning black.' The sunglasses slipped down on his nose. The pyramid finally collapsed in the blaze but the can remained centered in the inferno. '*Spray nozzle beginning to ignite like a candle.*' Or maybe like a cherry bomb fuse, Marcus wondered. Would the nozzle start sizzling like a firecracker and then blow into smithereens?

One minute passed, then two. The flames began to die. The plastic nozzle disintegrated. Marcus could not be patient much longer, which was not a positive trait for a scientist. Marcus peered around through the truck's windows to detect any nosy neighbors. The coast was clear.

Maybe he should add more lighter fluid, he thought. Then again, what if the can exploded as soon as he accessed ground zero? Although it would be for a noble cause, he did not want to be a famous dead scientist.

Marcus waited longer. The last flame shrunk and died. Before Marcus could sense the disappointment of his failure, a giant KA-BLAM resounded throughout the neighborhood. The loud blast startled him as the can shot straight up into the sky. Three silent seconds passed as the can raced back down and bounced off his dad's truck hood. The sunglasses dangled from one of his ears.

Marcus survived unhurt, but his dad's car suffered a large dent that would certainly be noticed the next time he drove it. Marcus would be grounded for life.

Marcus jumped out of the truck and kicked the hot-busted can closer to the extinguished fire pit. He shrugged his shoulders as nosy Miss Jenkins peeked her head out her back door.

The damage to the truck appeared even worse from the outside. He had to think of an excuse.

Marcus made a final entry in the binder:

'Hairspray can exploded. Scared flying bird carrying large rock. Bird dropped rock onto truck.'

The Apple Man

"Look mom, it's the Apple Man again," a trick-or-treater said as he passed Mr. Martin Willobee on the street for the second time.

"I think you'd better eat that yourself, it's very nutritious," a little princess smirked.

"Is that a Fuji?" a tiny pirate sneered as he passed with his mom. Martin dared not answer, for he didn't have a monster voice.

"So...how old are you?" the little princess asked, "like one hundred years old?" Martin pointed up, signaling he was much older.

"Two hundred?"

Martin nodded unmonsterlylike, then stretched out his arm, the fresh apple dangling in his fingers.

"Don't take it mom!" a little hobo warned. "It's poisonous!"

Now that was the reaction Martin was looking for. There was

just something downright evil about a frumpy, hunched man with a scary mask offering a shiny apple to children. 'Here, little girl,' he would mumble. The mother fixed a silent gaze on Martin. Was that horror he detected in her eyes? Even with no fangs or claws or dripping blood, Martin was the terror of the neighborhood. He angled his arm further out and slowly rotated the tempting fruit with his fingertips.

"I read about you in a story," the little hobo said. "Stay away from him, mom."

Martin managed a hysterical cackle to add drama.

"Do you live here on Palm Street?" The mom asked without fear. It would have spoiled the moment if he told her he was the new neighbor and lived in the house directly behind him. After all, he was the Apple Man. He should live in an enchanted apple forest. He lied by shaking his head. "Oh well, you are creepy, in a good way, of course," she said. "Have a Happy Halloween." Then she left with her little hobo.

As Martin turned back to his house, he saw his new wife, Dorma, dropping several home-made chocolate truffles into a dozen begging baskets. She stood in the middle of the walkway with a crazy clown hat and big shoes. 'Make sure you eat the truffles, you cute little rats,' he heard her say. He didn't think Dorma really liked kids, and considered them more as distractions in their relationship. Martin loved kids, and always found ways to be a ball catcher, a hide-and-seeker, or a Santa depending on the occasion. To Dorma, kids were mostly a nuisance that made unnecessary noises and trampled her flowers. Tonight, on the other hand, he was happy that Dorma was enthusiastic about entertaining the children.

Martin curled his back and limped in the middle of the street. A car approached slowly with bright beams. He outstretched an arm, seducing the driver with his Red Delicious. As the vehicle stopped next to him, he saw a mom and dad in the front and two excited trick-or-treaters in the back. Probably the family was searching for a neighborhood that was offering the best chocolates to the hungry goblins.

"Look kids, he wants to give you an apple," the mom spoke like he was an old friend. "Go ahead, take it, Carlos."

From out of nowhere a little masked man with a cape emerged from the back seat and grabbed the fruit from Martin's hand. "Uhmm, yummy apple," he said in a sinister voice. He stuffed it in his candy-filled pillowcase and proceeded down the street with his witch sister behind him.

Defeated, Martin returned to his house. One of Dorma's chocolate truffles must have fallen on the ground because he could see the reflection of its cellophane from the glow of the Jack-O-Lantern in the damp grass. He lifted it, removed its shiny covering, and stuffed the dark candy into the mouth hole of his mask. The dark chocolate tasted bitter, and almost burned as it oozed down his throat.

"Are you having a good time, my love?" Dorma said as she opened the front door. "Did someone take your poisoned apple?"

"Mmnph, yeah," Martin swallowed hard. "Batman stole it."

"See? That's what happens when you offer things to greedy kids." Dorma spoke in a lower-than-normal voice. Her eyes were glassy and gazed straight through him. "Now we can finally be alone without those little rats, my love." Martin realized something evil had happened to Dorma. A eerie tingle crawled up his back when he saw an opened box reading *Rat Poison* by the leftover truffles and basket of apples. "If you need more apples I prepared more of them on the table where I made the truffles."

The Stolen Car

Grant Gomez should have known something was wrong when he approached his old Nissan Maxima in the dark holiday-lighted parking lot. But he didn't.

He was sure the cost of gasoline to drive to the mall drugstore was more than the price of a tiny bottle of a cholesterol-reducing drug he needed. The doctor told him he could eliminate his pizza diet, or take a tiny miracle pill that would allow him to eat an extra slice.

The key fit perfectly into the door slot and turned with the familiar ca-chuk sound. Grant dropped into the cushy seat, slung the pharmacy bag to the passenger side, and reinserted the key into the ignition. The steering wheel seemed sticky and the grip felt foreign. Before turning the key, he noticed a pile of coats in the back. His wife and daughter must have used the Maxima for their last shopping expedition and forgot to bring them back inside the house. Although the car was old, he did not appreciate his family members turning it into a traveling motel.

The key turned smoothly and the engine started with ease. One knows the sounds and squeaks of their automobiles, and the Maxima purred as he remembered. Headlights on, check.

Sealtbelts clamped, check. Pull driveshaft into.... Wait a minute. The dashboard lit up brighter than normal. 155,000 miles on the odometer? He could have sworn it was no more than 90,000. Guess it was about time for a trade-in. Then again, time passes quickly, and maybe he hadn't checked it for a few years. His paranoia ceased, for it would be impossible for his keys to unlock the door and start the car if it belonged to someone else.

Pull driveshaft into reverse. Wait. Something wasn't right. Grant's seat seemed a little lower and farther back. He had only been taking the medicine for two weeks. Was shrinking a side effect? Also, every car has a unique smell. Grant detected a woodsy aroma coming from somewhere. Probably from Camilla and Madison's girl junk they threw in the back seat. Was this his car? The blinking drugstore light saying, 'Santa's Savings' could not cut through the darkness. Grant decided to settle this once and for all. He stretched to open the glove compartment. The small, yellow light glowed warmly, illuminating years of important trash and wrinkled papers that nearly spilled onto the floorboard. Yep, this was indeed old Bessie.

As the vehicle rolled out from the parking lot, Grant noticed a slight twisted, bumpy-like movement. Bad news, he thought. A flat tire.

He got out, walked around the vehicle, and inspected each tire. Other than needing a desperate wash and few dings that needed repaired, the tires appeared inflated. Camilla always told him to keep the AAA membership because one of these days the Maxima would break down in the middle of the road. Maybe it was time to buy a new one, but the faithful tan car always safely transported them from Point A to Point B. He hopped back in and heard the familiar swish of air as his buttocks plopped into the bucket seat.

On the main road, Grant prepared his speech for his family to re-hang their coats back in the closet. That lecture could wait, for his stomach growled, and he knew Camilla threw a pepperoni and mushroom into the oven before he left. He did remember when he once accidentally got into a wrong car. The door was unlocked, and he was greeted by a large bag of strange groceries in the passenger seat. He looked both ways, and quietly got out and slid into his own car parked close by. But tonight he was driving *his* car and it started to feel more and more like his cozy living room.

Nearing home, Grant peered down at the radio. It was the standard unit that came with all Maximas. However, just four months ago he installed a new Sonic MusicBlaster! Was he going crazy? Did someone reinstall the old radio as a prank? He was driving a stolen vehicle. He was a thief! Was he hallucinating? He glanced around and his eyes stopped at the half-opened console. There was a little white bottle with a blue ship. He raised it into the air with a free hand and it said Old Spice cologne. Not his brand. For certain, he was now a criminal, a fugitive on the run, and driving to his own house where there would already be five or six police cars with blinking lights. What would the neighbors think? How would he explain that to Camilla? He had to return the car immediately without being noticed.

From out of nowhere, Grant was overwhelmed with a feeling of freedom. He was actually driving someone else's car. That was awesome! How many times does a person have the opportunity to drive a strange vehicle without the owner's permission? It was like having a new car. But then again, his car had 60,000 fewer miles, so it was not a fair trade.

'Hey babe, hop in,' he would tell Camilla when he got home. 'How do you like my new wheels?' He could have a lot of fun with that. But wait. Since his key fit into this car, wouldn't another key fit into his own car? Was the owner, or the entire holiday shopping family, now taking a driving spree with old Bessie? If so, they were enjoying a smoother ride while splitting their ears with his new Sonic MusicBlaster.

Grant sniffed the cologne at the red light, and splashed two handfuls of the zesty liquid onto his neck before making a U-turn. Would there be police at the scene, waiting to shoot or arrest him once he was identified? What if the owners saw him pull their car back into the stall? Grant could see it in his brain. 'Look, Dad, that man is stealing your car!'

After two revolutions Grant discovered his Maxima where he left it. But how could he go back and simply re-park the car? If he did, the owners would find their car like nothing happened, pile their Christmas goodies into the back and go about their daily lives. His once-in-a-lifetime adventure would not alter history. Grant parked the old car four rows away from where he found it, slanted it diagonally to consume three parking places, and heaved the front tire on top of the concrete curb by the shopping carts.

Today he still wonders what the family thought when they found their car that night? Did the driver think someone tried to steal his car but had a change of heart? Did he make sure no one rummaged the pockets of the coats for money? Or did he have the same hallucinations as Grant? Did he think, 'Maybe I did park my car crazily in three stalls next to the shopping carts?'

The Weird Bug

Brayden Boswell was already tense from reading the book, "Creepy Insects of the World," so he didn't think about the tickle he felt on his left arm close to his shoulder. Celeste was on his other side watching some kind of alien movie. He felt it again in the same spot, then calmly moved the book over and raised his head back to focus on his arm. Sure enough, there was the tiniest blur of a moving object. Brayden placed his head into a position to focus his glasses onto the small, gray spot. He gazed through his bifocals to get a close up. The bug appeared to have six legs, with its front two arms reaching up like a miniature praying mantis. Surely a creature so small could do no harm, he thought. *"Aliens have now attacked the major metropolitan center of Chicago,"* the TV blared as Celeste was munching on Snack Crisps.

"Celeste," Brayden said. "Look at this weird bug."

"Just a minute, this is the good part."

Brayden returned his head back in an awkward position to focus sharply on the uninvited guest. As he squinted, he could see the creature making human-like animations. First, it probed his arm with its right forearm, and then repeated the behavior with its other arm. Peering closer, it appeared the non-winged creature was actually contemplating the skin samples it was conducting. It moved its head independently from its arms, and seemed to approve of its scientific findings. Then its head twisted and looked directly at Brayden with two microscopic eyes. He was positive the life-form was aware of his presence. It raised its antennae upward and together and pointed them towards his nose. Brayden swore he detected a tiny beam of light emitting from the end of the antennae.

"Aliens eject a microscopic species of life in residential area!" Celeste had her full attention on the TV and almost missed her lips as she attempted to insert another Snack Crisp into her mouth.

"Celeste, look!" Brayden said louder, pointing to his arm.

"What? You always bother me when I'm watching TV."

"No, really. You have super close-up vision. Put this thing in a jar so we can see what the heck it is!"

"Eww, looks like a spider." Smack! Celeste slapped his arm with a magazine and squished the creature into an unrecognizable dot of gray liquid.

"Why did you do that?" he complained.

"Don't like any spiders in the house. And I sure don't want any crawling on the ceiling while we are sleeping."

"Scientist calling the new life-form 'gray scavengers,'" the TV said. "Some humans have been inflicted with sharp laser stings from their antennae."

The Diamond Sale

Travis Tweedle felt a sort of uneasiness as he sat facing Drew Damon across from the small wooden table in the diamond room. The diamond room was a soundproof, two-person chamber intended to be a private area that stood cozily in the corner of his jewelry store, but when two men are negotiating the sale of a half-million dollar gem, the small quarters could quickly become uncomfortable.

Drew was a large man anyway, and his knees had already bumped Travis' on two occasions. His hands were thick from working his entire life at the large printing company he now owned. He certainly could have afforded nicer clothes and even the diamond merchant's entire jewelry company, but Drew had a down-home style that was both gruff and likable.

Grasping the diamond with metallic tweezers, Drew held the humongous stone up to the light. It would be impossible for any human being, no matter what their profession, to ignore this giant kaleidoscope that was created a million years ago by the forces of nature. Splattered patterns of vivid colors spewed upon the walls of the diamond room.

"There's a flaw on the edge," Drew said with a poker face after he had already painfully whittled the price down to $490,000.

"That's correct," Travis answered. "It is nature's way of saying it is real. The flaw will never get bigger or smaller, and will remain there as an identifying characteristic for the next million years."

"Can you discount the stone for the flaw?" Travis noticed a micro smile coming from the left corner of Drew's lips. He was very educated about diamonds and knew that such a diamond without an inclusion would appraise for a quarter million higher.

"Drew," Travis said with a friendly smile. "The small inclusion will be completely concealed by the prong of the ring. Unless you are looking for it, you will never see it. In fact, I'm not going to charge you one dollar extra for this beautiful flaw."

Drew's left corner of his lip rose slightly higher. It is important, in any sales situation, that the buyer likes his diamond merchant to some degree. Of course trust is ninety-five percent of the industry, and Drew purchased many smaller items from Travis in the past.

"Travis, what do you think she'll say when I give this to her?"

Being in the diamond business since he delivered jewelry repairs for a New Albany store as a kid, Travis was prepared for that question. Since the beginning of time, diamonds given to a lover have always been an emotional purchase. He always hoped that the relationship symbolized by the stone lasted for a very long time. Drew always had many girlfriends, but confessed that his new girl was the woman of his dreams. "Drew, just make sure Barbinda is close to a soft couch when she opens the box," Travis began. "Because I have a feeling she may faint."

"You didn't answer my question, Travis. How do I know she will say yes?"

"Drew," Travis had his rebuttal memorized, "I can guarantee the quality of the diamond in your hand, but I cannot guarantee the romance." Travis held a smile throughout his reply and paused. It was never the best close, but it was true. He lightly bit his lip and prayed that Drew did not detect the tiny drop of sweat that dripped down from the center of his forehead onto his nose. The diamond room was already stuffy because the air conditioner was not working properly and Drew's large body generated heat. "How did you want to take care of the paperwork, Drew?"

Drew became quiet, and didn't respond for what seemed like an eternity. Travis kept silent. The first one to speak loses. "If you weren't such a damn nice guy, Travis," Drew muttered. Then he lifted a shaggy briefcase that he kept close to his leg. Here's a check for $200,000 and $90,000 in greenbacks as a deposit. I'll give you the rest after you set the stone. Don't worry, Travis. The money is real. I just printed it this morning." Drew showed his largest smile of the day. Travis supposed the counterfeit money joke was standard for anyone in the printing business.

He ambled up from the small chair and shook the diamond merchant's hand. Travis's small fingers disappeared within Drew's grasp.

"Thank you, Travis." Drew said as he turned around to leave. He paused. "Can I ask you a favor?"

"Sure, Drew," Travis said.

"Will you please use this money to buy a bigger building, perhaps with a larger diamond room?"

"Yes sir." he said.

The Blade of Grass

You may analyze my brain
To see what is inside
You might think I am disturbed
With thoughts I cannot hide

When I behold this blade of grass
All things I understand
Life revealed before our eyes
Within a single strand

I once held a jar of fish
Their colors splashed for all to see
Watch them dashing up and down
A masterpiece to me

A micro world of wonder seen
Flashing shiny blue and green
Lashing through their liquid world
Metallic fins they swirled

Then it crashed upon the rocks
The scorching ground was way too hot
Thrashing wildly in their shock
For their lives they really fought

Living poems in a glass
Once contained within my clasp
No one cared about their fraught
Or the lesson that was taught

I still see their colors splash
When I behold this blade of grass

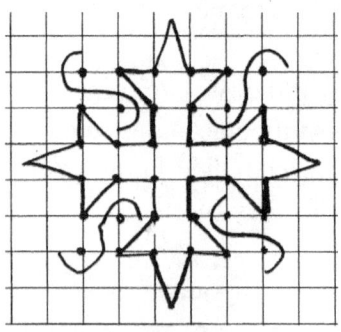

This magical symbol can be drawn easily
by using a square graph of thirty-six dots.

www.ingramcontent.com/pod-product-compliance
Lightning Source LLC
Chambersburg PA
CBHW020625130626
46552CB00003B/1099